WILDERNESS GUIDEBOOK

DETROIT PUBLIC LIBRARY

P9-EFJ-358

CHASE BRANCH LIBRARY
17731 W. SEVEN MILE RD.
DETROIT, MI 48235
578-8002

SEP - - 2014

CH

CAMP
REX

by

Molly Idle

VIKING

An Imprint of Penguin Group (USA)

Searching for an outing to enjoy with your friends?
Consider camping!

The fresh air and exercise are invigorating!

Remember to stay together as a group . . .

and stick to the trail.

When you reach the campsite, find the perfect place to pitch your tent.

Once you've made camp,
you can explore the
surrounding area. . . .

Learning about the local flora and fauna can be great fun!

So long as you take care to avoid any dangerous plants . . .

and refrain from disturbing the natural landscape . . .

or its inhabitants.

If the opportunity presents itself, there's nothing more refreshing
than a dip in a mountain lake or a bit of canoeing.

You may even catch a fish or two for supper.

After all, the seasoned camper enjoys gathering wood, kindling a flame,

and cooking over a properly prepared campfire.

A traditional sing-along and marshmallow roast always bring campers closer together.

Telling spooky stories can be fun, too, until it's time to turn in.

Before you fall asleep, it's lovely to listen to the
soothing sounds of the forest all around you.

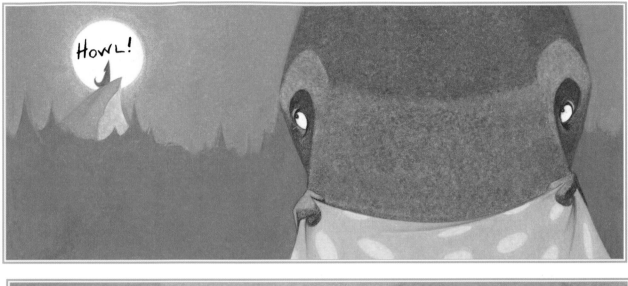

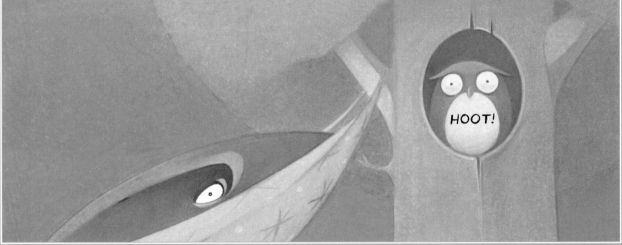

In the morning, you'll awake refreshed . . .

and ready to head out on the trail again.

For experienced campers are as much at home
in the great outdoors . . .

as they are in their own backyard.

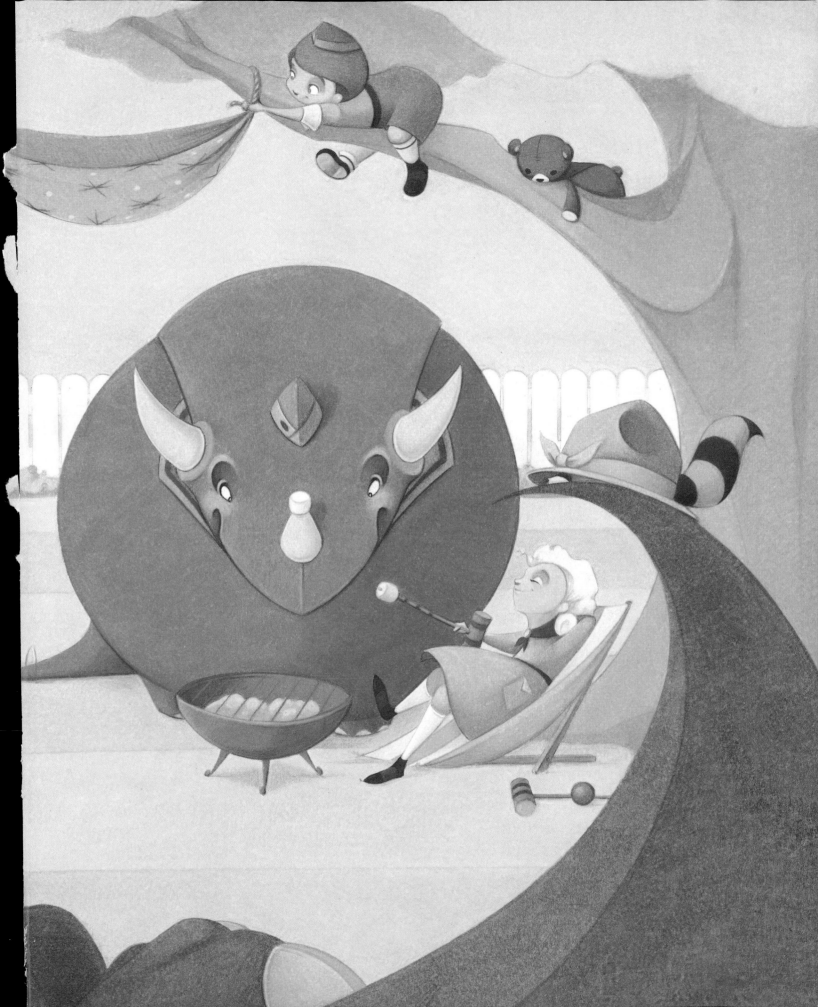

For Denise, Nancy, and Tracy

VIKING

Published by the Penguin Group

Penguin Group (USA) LLC

375 Hudson Street

New York, New York 10014

USA ✦ Canada ✦ UK ✦ Ireland ✦ Australia ✦ New Zealand ✦ India ✦ South Africa ✦ China

penguin.com

A Penguin Random House Company

First published in the United States of America by Viking, an imprint of Penguin Young Readers Group, 2014

Copyright © 2014 by Molly Idle

Penguin supports copyright. Copyright fuels creativity, encourages diverse voices, promotes free speech, and creates a vibrant culture. Thank you for buying an authorized edition of this book and for complying with copyright laws by not reproducing, scanning, or distributing any part of it in any form without permission. You are supporting writers and allowing Penguin to continue to publish books for every reader.

LIBRARY OF CONGRESS CATALOGING-IN-PUBLICATION DATA

Idle, Molly.

Camp Rex / by Molly Idle.

pages cm

Summary: Cordelia and her troop of dino-scouts enjoy a camping trip in the great outdoors.

ISBN 978-0-670-78573-5 (hardcover)

[1. Tyrannosaurus rex—Fiction. 2. Dinosaurs—Fiction. 3. Camping—Fiction. 4. Scouting (Youth activity)—Fiction. 5. Humorous stories.] I. Title.

PZ7.I217Cam 2014   [E]—dc23   2013018234

Manufactured in China

1 3 5 7 9 10 8 6 4 2

Book design by Nancy Brennan   Set in F Caslon Twelve